DEDICATED TO LOUIS & OTIS

FATHER PENGUIN AND MOTHER PENGUIN WERE WORKING VERY HARD TO PUT THE DECORATIONS UP FOR CHRISTMAS.

"I'M NOT SURE THIS TREE IS GOING TO FIT," SAID FATHER PENGUIN. "DID WE HAVE TO GO FOR THE BIGGEST ONE IN THE SHOP?"

"I KNOW, I KNOW," MOTHER PENGUIN REPLIED. "BUT IT WILL LOOK AMAZING ONCE ALL OF THE DECORATIONS ARE ON IT!"

BROTHER PENGUIN AND LITTLE PENGUIN WERE PLAYING IN THEIR ROOM. THEY WERE DISCUSSING WHAT THEY WANTED FATHER CHRISTMAS TO BRING THEM ON CHRISTMAS DAY.

"I WOULD REALLY LIKE A BRAND-NEW SHINY HAIRBRUSH," SAID BROTHER PENGUIN. "THE ONE I HAVE IS OLD AND A BIT WORN OUT. WHAT WOULD YOU LIKE FOR CHRISTMAS, LITTLE PENGUIN?"

"I WISH FATHER CHRISTMAS WOULD BRING ME A GALLON OF MILK," LITTLE PENGUIN REPLIED. LITTLE PENGUIN LOVED DRINKING MILK. SO MUCH SO THAT HE HAD THE WHITEST TEETH YOU HAVE EVER SEEN.

BROTHER PENGUIN LIKED TO LINE UP ALL HIS TOYS IN A ROW. HE ALSO LIKED TO MAKE SURE THEY WENT FROM SMALLEST TO LARGEST.

THERE WERE SOME THINGS THAT BROTHER PENGUIN NEEDED HELP WITH. THINGS LIKE TYING HIS SHOELACES AND BRUSHING HIS PENGUIN HAIR.

ALTHOUGH HE MAY HAVE FOUND THESE THINGS DIFFICULT, HE ALWAYS TRIED HIS BEST.

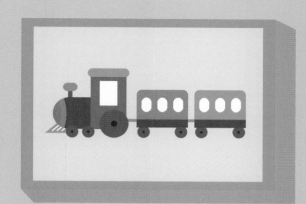

IT WAS A COUPLE OF DAYS BEFORE CHRISTMAS AND LITTLE PENGUIN SAW BROTHER PENGUIN BRUSHING HIS HAIR. IT WAS PROVING TO BE QUITE DIFFICULT.

"WOULD YOU LIKE ME TO HELP YOU, BROTHER PENGUIN?" LITTLE PENGUIN ASKED.

BROTHER PENGUIN WAS VERY GRATEFUL FOR LITTLE PENGUIN'S HELP.

FATHER PENGUIN AND MOTHER PENGUIN WALKED PAST AND SAW THAT LITTLE PENGUIN WAS HELPING BROTHER PENGUIN TO BRUSH HIS HAIR.

"THAT'S VERY HELPFUL OF YOU, LITTLE PENGUIN," MOTHER PENGUIN SAID. "FATHER CHRISTMAS WILL BE VERY PLEASED THAT YOU'RE BEING SO KIND."

IT WAS NOW CHRISTMAS EVE AND BOTH BROTHER PENGUIN AND LITTLE PENGUIN WERE VERY, VERY EXCITED.

"I WONDER IF FATHER CHRISTMAS WILL BRING ME MY GALLON OF MILK," LITTLE PENGUIN SAID.

"I AM NOT SURE IF FATHER CHRISTMAS BRINGS MILK FOR CHILDREN, LITTLE PENGUIN," MOTHER PENGUIN SAID.

"BUT I HAVE BEEN A GOOD BOY THIS YEAR AND HELPED MY BROTHER BRUSH HIS HAIR EVERY DAY!" LITTLE PENGUIN SAID. HE WAS UNSURE WHETHER HE WOULD GET THAT BIG BOTTLE OF MILK.

BROTHER PENGUIN WAS WORRIED. HE REALLY HOPED LITTLE PENGUIN WOULD GET WHAT HE WANTED FOR CHRISTMAS, BECAUSE LITTLE PENGUIN WAS ALWAYS SO HELPFUL TO HIM WITH THE THINGS HE FOUND DIFFICULT. LIKE TYING HIS SHOELACES AND BRUSHING HIS PENGUIN HAIR.

"I KNOW!" THOUGHT BROTHER PENGUIN. "I WILL USE SOME OF MY BIRTHDAY MONEY AND GET LITTLE PENGUIN THAT GALLON OF MILK FOR CHRISTMAS!"

HE ASKED FATHER PENGUIN TO QUICKLY TAKE HIM TO THE GROCERY SHOP.

IT WAS CHRISTMAS MORNING AND THE PENGUIN FAMILY WERE
ALL SAT AROUND THE CHRISTMAS TREE OPENING THEIR PRESENTS.
"WOW! A RADIO!" CHEERED FATHER PENGUIN. "I MUST HAVE BEEN
GOOD THIS YEAR!"

"OH, LOOK! I'VE GOT A NEW WATCH!" MOTHER PENGUIN SAID. SHE
WAS VERY HAPPY.

"LOOK! LOOK!" SAID BROTHER PENGUIN. "FATHER CHRISTMAS HAS
GOT ME A BRAND-NEW HAIRBRUSH! I CAN'T WAIT FOR US TO USE
THIS, LITTLE PENGUIN!"

LITTLE PENGUIN HAD OPENED ALL OF HIS PRESENTS FROM FATHER
CHRISTMAS AND HE HAD LOTS OF LOVELY NEW TOYS TO PLAY WITH.

"YOU WERE RIGHT, MOTHER PENGUIN," SAID LITTLE PENGUIN. "FATHER CHRISTMAS DOESN'T BRING MILK FOR CHILDREN, DOES HE? IT'S OK, THOUGH. I HAVE BEEN VERY LUCKY TO GET WHAT I HAVE BEEN GIVEN."

"WAIT!" BROTHER PENGUIN SHOUTED. "I HAVE ONE MORE SPECIAL GIFT FOR YOU!"

WITH THE MONEY HE HAD LEFT OVER FROM HIS BIRTHDAY, BROTHER PENGUIN HAD BOUGHT LITTLE PENGUIN EXACTLY WHAT HE WANTED: A GALLON OF MILK!

"THIS IS AMAZING!" LITTLE PENGUIN SAID. HE WAS OVERWHELMED WITH THE KINDNESS OF BROTHER PENGUIN. THEY GAVE EACH OTHER A HUGE HUG.

LITTLE PENGUIN OPENED THE CARD BROTHER PENGUIN HAD STUCK ON THE GALLON OF MILK. THE CARD READ...

Dear Little Penguin,

Thank you for helping me every day.

If it wasn't for you I wouldn't be able to tie my shoelaces and brush my hair.

I hope you enjoy your Gallon of Milk. Merry Christmas

Love Brother Penguin x

Printed in Poland
by Amazon Fulfillment
Poland Sp. z o.o., Wrocław